# Babe

## The Film Storybook

# Babe

## The Film Storybook

Adapted by Ron Fontes and Justine Korman
From a screenplay by George Miller and Chris Noonan
Based on the novel *The Sheep-Pig* by Dick King-Smith

PUFFIN BOOKS

PUFFIN BOOKS

Published by the Penguin Group
Penguin Books Ltd, 27 Wrights Lane, London W8 5TZ, England
Penguin Books USA Inc., 375 Hudson Street, New York, New York 10014, USA
Penguin Books Australia Ltd, Ringwood, Victoria, Australia
Penguin Books Canada Ltd, 10 Alcorn Avenue, Toronto, Ontario, Canada M4V 3B2
Penguin Books (NZ) Ltd, 182–190 Wairau Road, Auckland 10, New Zealand

Penguin Books Ltd, Registered Offices: Harmondsworth, Middlesex, England

First published in the USA by Random House Inc.
Published in Great Britain in Puffin Books 1995
10 9 8 7 6 5 4 3

Copyright © MCA Publishing Rights, a division of MCA Inc., 1995
All rights reserved

Puffin Film and TV tie-in edition first published 1995

Filmset in Garamond 3

Made and printed in Great Britain by William Clowes Ltd, Beccles and London

*Reeeeeee-reee-screeee!* The tiny piglet squealed with all his might. Rough hands put him back in the cardboard box beneath a sign that said GUESS MY WEIGHT.

It had been a day full of changes for the small pig. In the morning his mother was put in a lorry marked GREEN VALLEY MEATS. The piglet was told that she was going to Paradise. But he missed her when he had to eat his breakfast from a metal tube. Later he was dropped into a sack. He was carried to a noisy place called a country fair and put in a box. Strange people kept lifting him up and putting him back down. The frightened piglet didn't like it at all.

'So what about it, Arthur? Fifty pence to guess his weight. Money goes to a good cause. And Christmas Day – think of the feast!' said Mr Thames of the Lions Club.

'Good-oh,' replied the quiet voice of Arthur Hogget.

Gentle fingers stroked the piglet between the ears. The piglet looked up. His bright eyes met the farmer's calm gaze. He was lifted by hands as steady and warm as rocks in the sun. The hands were gentle, despite their strength. The little pig relaxed.

'Funny, that. It's the first time all day he hasn't screamed to high heaven,' Mr Thames observed.

Balancing the little piglet in one hand, Mr Hogget dropped his coins on to the money tray. He held the pig thoughtfully. 'Twelve pounds...' The piglet nuzzled the farmer's cheek. '...Ar...three ounces,' Hogget concluded. He patted the piglet one more time and gently returned him to the box.

'*Hoo-eee!* Hogget!' Mrs Hogget's voice rang out over the clamour of the fair. She was as loud and round and practical as her husband was quiet and lean and dreamy. She waved a silver trophy and a hand full of blue ribbons for best jams and jellies.

Hogget turned from the booth and went to meet his wife.

'We'll be weighing the little chap tomorrow,' Mr Thames called after him. 'We'll phone if you win.'

'Righty-oh,' Hogget said softly.

*Screeee-reeee-reee!* The piglet started shrieking again as another pair of hands lifted him from the box.

The next day, the piglet saw the kind farmer again. This time, Hogget picked him up and took him to his farm. He put the small pink pig in a pen in a barn. Hogget had won the contest – he had guessed the piglet's weight exactly.

Three black-and-white puppies named Skip, Trip, and Dash stared over a low wall of hay bales.

'What is it?' Skip asked.

'It's called a pig,' said Fly, the mother sheepdog.

'The Bosses will eat it when it's big enough,' Trip guessed.

'Will they eat us when we're big, too?' Dash wondered.

'Good heavens, no!' Fly answered. 'The Bosses eat only stupid animals, like sheep and ducks and chickens.'

'Are pigs stupid?' asked Skip.

Fly looked at the piglet's white-furred face with its funny pink snout. Actually, she'd never known a pig before, but she certainly didn't want

to seem at all ignorant in front of her children, so she said, 'Not as stupid as sheep, but definitely stupid.'

'Excuse me. No, we're not,' whispered the piglet in a quavering voice.

Fly was shocked that the odd creature had spoken to her. 'Good heavens. Who are you?'

'I'm a Large White,' said the piglet.

Skip laughed. 'Gosh! What's a small one like?'

'I expect that's your breed, dear. What's your name?' Fly asked.

The piglet had never been asked that before. 'I don't know.'

The puppies dissolved in laughter. This stupid animal didn't even know his own name!

'Well,' said Fly, 'what did your mother call you to tell you apart from your brothers and sisters?'

Tears choked the tiny piglet's throat. No pig ever came back from Paradise. He would never see his mother again. He finally answered in a trembling voice, 'Our mother called us all the same – Babe.'

Skip, Trip, and Dash giggled, but Fly's heart went out to this odd, lonely beast. 'That's a lovely name, dear,' she said kindly. 'Why don't we call you that? It'll make you feel more at home.'

Babe burst into tears. 'I want my Mum!' he wailed.

Fly jumped over the hay bales. 'There, there, dear. You've got to be a brave boy now. I left my mother when I was your age, and my pups will leave me soon. But I'll keep an eye on you, if you like.' She licked Babe's nose. 'There, is that nice?'

Babe snuggled against the sheepdog's warm fur. Then a shadow fell across the pen. Everyone looked up to see Rex, the grand old sheepdog who was king of Hogget's farm. Rex looked down disapprovingly.

'The little fellow's a bit low,' Fly explained. 'He's going to sleep with us. Just till he finds his feet,' she added hastily.

Rex said nothing for a moment. But he was not pleased. He did not look kindly on dogs mixing with lesser animals.

A giddy cow chanted, 'Pigs is pigs and dogs is dogs. Isn't that right, Rex?'

The big dog glared at her. Then Rex turned to Fly and said, 'Until he finds his feet.'

 *Quack-a-doodle-doo!*

The next morning, Babe was snuggled up against Fly when he heard the strange sound. It was Ferdinand the duck, crowing with all his might to greet the dawn before the cockerel had his chance. The puppies told Babe that Ferdinand was 'off his rocker'.

'We'll catch him and eat him one day, won't we, Mum?' Dash said.

Fly yawned. 'Yes, dear. Now come along.'

The dogs left the barn and went to the farmhouse for their breakfast. Babe waddled after them. But Fly stopped the piglet before he could push through the doggy door. 'You wait here, Babe.'

'Aren't pigs allowed?' he asked.

Trip giggled. 'Not live ones!'

'Only dogs and cats inside the house,' Fly said gently.

'Why?' Babe asked.

Fly didn't know. 'That's just the way things are,' she said.

The same thing happened later when Babe tried to follow the sheep-dogs to the fields. 'Not you, dear,' Fly said at the gate.

'Why?' Babe asked.

'We have to help the Boss look after his sheep,' Fly replied. 'That's dogs' work. You're a pig. Your job's to stay here and eat your food. We'll be back at the end of the day.'

Babe was very confused. He didn't even know what a sheep was. He looked around the busy farmyard. Hens bustled in their coop. Ducks washed in the pond. And no one paid the slightest attention to him.

Then he heard something new. *Baaaaah. Baaah.* He trotted off to investigate.

Babe discovered the sound was coming from a covered pen. He

couldn't see inside. But he heard a hoarse voice complaining, 'Darn wolf! Never do leave a body alone. Nag, nag, naaaag, all day long. Go here, go there, do this, do that.' The voice broke into a fit of coughing.

'I'm not a wolf,' Babe said.

'Oh, I knows all that. Calls yourself a sheepdog. But you don't fool none of us,' the voice replied.

'I'm not a sheepdog, either.' Babe moved to look through a gap between the planks of the pen.

'Well, I'll be dipped! What are you?' the voice demanded.

'Pig. Large White. What are you?' Babe asked.

'Ewe,' the voice replied.

Babe was confused for a moment. But then he had a thought. 'You're a sheep!' he cried.

The old sheep nodded her woolly head. 'The name's Maa. And I'm stuck in this little box till the Boss makes me well again.'

'What's wrong with you, Maa?' Babe asked politely.

The old sheep held up a foreleg. 'Foot rot. And I've got a nasty cough. And I'm not as young as I used to be.'

'You don't look very old to me,' Babe said.

'Too kind. First kind word I've heard in donkey's years,' Maa said with a sigh. 'You seem a nice young chap, not like them wolves. Treat you like dirt, they do. Bite you as soon as look at you, the savages.'

'Bite you?' Babe shuddered.

'And worse,' Maa continued. 'Much worse.'

'Fly would never be mean,' Babe said.

'Who's that?' Maa asked.

'She's my mo – ' he began, then blushed. 'She's the she-dog here.'

'Fly, is it?' Maa coughed. 'Black and white? Teeth sharp as a steel trap?' Babe nodded.

'All them wolves is cruel to us sheep. Always have been. No brains, no heart.' Maa coughed again. 'Wouldn't want to see a gentle soul like you mixing with the likes of them.'

Now Babe was more mixed up than ever. Was his new mother really bad?

That evening, when Fly came in from the fields, she gave Babe's face a big, slurpy kiss. As he nuzzled against her, Babe decided that the old sheep must be wrong. Maybe Maa was confused because she was sick. Babe hoped she would get better soon.

The next morning, Babe woke to yet another strange sound. *Ba-riiiiinggg*. Mrs Hogget had got tired of the rooster and Ferdinand out-cock-a-doodling each other. So she had bought an alarm clock.

When the Hoggets were at church, Ferdinand sidled up to Babe.

'You look like an intelligent young fellow,' the duck said. 'I need your help with a simple matter.'

Ferdinand whispered his plan to Babe. Babe listened very carefully. He was flattered that the duck wanted his help. Finally, Babe had something more important to do than just eat!

Ferdinand led Babe to the door. 'Let's go over it one more time,' he said.

Babe recited dutifully, 'I go through the kitchen, across the living-room...'

'How do you go across the living-room?' Ferdinand asked.

'Quietly, so I don't wake up the cat,' Babe said. 'Then into the bedroom, get the mechanical rooster, and bring it to you.' All of a sudden Babe thought of something. 'But it's against the rules. Only dogs and cats are allowed in the house.'

'It's a good rule,' Ferdinand agreed. 'But this is a matter of life and death!'

Once again, poor Babe was confused. 'It is?'

Ferdinand sighed. 'Humans eat ducks, especially plump ones. Most ducks don't like to think about it, but it's a fact.'

Babe was shocked.

Ferdinand lifted a wing to show his ribs. 'That's why I keep thin. That's my first rule of survival in a cruel world. And the second rule is Be Indispensable.'

Babe didn't know what that big word meant.

'Be Useful!' Ferdinand cried. 'Humans don't eat cats. Why? Because they catch mice. Humans don't eat roosters because they wake everyone up in the morning. So I try crowing, and what happens? They bring in a machine to do the job. That's why you've got to get that mechanical rooster!'

'Why me?' Babe asked.

'Because I'm allergic to cats,' Ferdinand explained. Then he added, more quietly, 'My life is in your hands...er, trotters.'

Babe slipped quietly through the door and into the cosy farmhouse kitchen. At the entrance to the living-room, he paused to look

around. On the table was the doll's house Mr Hogget was building for his granddaughter. Beside the pots of paint and brushes sat Mrs Hogget's knitting basket. And on the hearth rug was Duchess, the Hoggets' big grey cat. Luckily, Duchess was still asleep.

Babe carefully made his way through the living-room. He did his best to stay as far away from Duchess as possible. Half-way across the room,

Babe had to squeeze between an armchair and a table leg. His chubby hips nudged the table, and a ball of wool rolled out of the knitting basket. It bounced across the armchair, off a lamp, and around a vase before it hit the floor.

Babe froze in horror as he realized the ball was rolling straight towards Duchess! Then, just before it touched the cat's silky paw, the wool stopped. Babe sighed. Then he continued his careful trek across the living-room.

After that, the piglet's bright eyes never strayed from the sleeping cat. But Babe was watching Duchess so carefully that he didn't notice that some of the wool had wrapped around one of his feet. With each step, the wool pulled tighter, tugging at the knitting basket, paint pots, the lamp, and the vase...

Ferdinand saw it all through the window. Before anything could fall, he quietly rushed through the door into the house. Babe stood like a statue while Ferdinand gently plucked the wool from around his hoof.

'Go outside,' the duck whispered in a nasal voice, choked with allergies. His eyes were watery and red.

'But you said you needed me,' Babe said.

'Well, then, stand guard,' Ferdinand whispered, heading for the bedroom.

Babe waited for a moment, then he followed Ferdinand.

'Guard what?' he asked.

Ferdinand let out a tortured groan. 'Forget it. Stick with me, and please – I beg you – not one more word.'

Ferdinand pushed the clock on to the bed and Babe picked it up in his mouth. Then together, they crept back into the living-room, past Duchess. The cat stretched sleepily and her claw snagged the yarn, which was still wrapped around the furniture. Ferdinand and Babe both held their breath.

Then a sneeze twitched in the duck's nose. 'Ah...Ahh...*Ahhh!*'

Babe's tail shot across Ferdinand's nostrils just in time. The two animals stood frozen for a while longer before heading on. They made it all the way to the door when suddenly – *Ah-choo!* – Ferdinand sneezed. Duchess immediately woke up. Her paw moved, pulling the yarn with a jerk. The farmhouse exploded with crashes, splashes, squeals, smashes, quacks, and a loud *Ba-ring!*

Rex had no trouble solving the mystery. Beside the broken alarm clock were two sets of footprints in bright paint. One set was red and webbed. The other set was pointy and blue.

Later, in the barn, the old sheepdog declared, 'From now on, we will all respect the rules. "To each creature its own destiny; every animal in its proper place." And a pig's place is in the mud-wallow by the pond. Not in the barn. And absolutely never in the house. Is that understood?'

Babe was too upset to nod. He was one very sorry, very blue pig.

Soon Babe was pink again. The puppies were sold to other farmers who needed sheepdogs. Rex had no patience with Fly's sorrow, but Mr Hogget patted her gently, and Babe licked her snout.

'Fly,' he said softly, 'may I call you Mum?'

Fly nuzzled the piglet tenderly. At last, Babe had truly found his place on Hogget's farm. As the nights grew longer and colder, Babe grew bigger. And crazy Ferdinand became more and more frantic. 'Christmas means carnage!' he raved. Babe didn't understand what the duck was screeching about, but he did notice that a lot of new and different things seemed to be happening.

First, Mr and Mrs Hogget's daughter, son-in-law, and grandchildren came to visit. The farmhouse was suddenly filled with all sorts of bright, shiny things. There was singing and laughter. And the people piled brightly wrapped boxes under a tree inside the house.

Then one day Mrs Hogget washed the mud off Babe and measured his taut belly with a tape measure. Babe didn't know what was happening. But Fly knew. She had seen other animals taken into the building near the barn. It was the way of nature, but that didn't stop her from feeling sad.

Before Fly left for the fields on Christmas Eve, she told Babe, 'I want you to have the most wonderful day you possibly can. Whatever happens, think only happy thoughts.'

Babe beamed. 'I'll try.'

Fly turned away before the young pig could see her tears.

Fly wasn't the only one feeling sad. Mr Hogget didn't want to say goodbye to the sweet-tempered pig, either. So he mentioned to Mrs Hogget that it would be a shame to miss out on first prize for Best Ham at next year's fair. He knew his wife had a weakness for blue ribbons. And sure enough, she changed the Christmas menu to duck à l'orange.

The duck wasn't skinny Ferdinand. But it was a duck Ferdinand knew well, and it was enough to make up his mind.

'I'm going away,' Ferdinand told Babe as they stood at the gate to the Hoggets' farm.

'Where?' the pig asked.

'I don't know,' said Ferdinand.

'But I'm a clever duck. I could do with an adventure.'

'I'll miss you, Ferdy,' Babe said softly.

'Ferdy!' the duck quacked happily. 'No one's ever called me that before.' Then he jumped up on the gate and turned to Babe. 'Good luck, Pig. Always remember: Fat Is Fatal!' And with that, he took off.

Babe watched Ferdinand become a black dot in the sky. Then he heard a faint sound of bleating. He scanned the green hills for the source of the bleating. He saw a flock of sheep, a lorry, strange men, and a dog. Babe trotted closer.

'*Wolf! Wolf!*' the flock bleated wildly.

Babe wriggled through the fence and ran across the field to join the frantic sheep. Woolly flanks pressed against him as the sheep were herded towards the truck.

Babe recognized his old friend. 'Maa!'

'Young 'un! You're alive!' Maa exclaimed.

'What's happening?' Babe asked. 'Who are these men? Our Boss isn't here. This doesn't seem right.'

'If I could say what went on in the minds of Men, wouldn't I be a wise old sheep!' Maa replied.

None of the animals knew much about Men. So naturally, they couldn't even imagine what a sheep rustler was. Babe decided to ask the strange dog why his masters were taking Hogget's flock. But instead of answering, the dog nipped the pig's tail!

Babe ran for his life, with the dog barking and snapping at his heels.

18

He wriggled back through the fence and ran squealing to the farmhouse.

Mr Hogget saw Fly's ears perk up at the sound. She started barking. Something was wrong! The farmer raced off in his lorry. The dogs ran across the fields.

Rex reached the other lorry first. It was still empty. The thieves slammed the tailgate shut and crashed through the fence at top speed.

Rex was still barking when Fly and Hogget arrived. They were followed by an exhausted Babe. Hogget patted Fly's head and said, 'Good dog.'

Fly jumped into the lorry bed. Then the farmer lifted Babe up beside her. 'Good pig,' he said.

That night it was all over the farm that Mr Hogget thought Babe was a watch-pig. Rex sulked because he hadn't heard Babe first. But Fly beamed as she licked Babe's wounded tail. 'I'm very proud of you, m'boy.'

'I'm going to be a good sheepdog when I grow up, aren't I?' Babe said.

Fly answered carefully. 'None of my pups would have done any better than you did today.'

The next morning, in the cosy farmhouse kitchen, the Hogget family looked over their Christmas presents. While his daughter and wife talked about the new fax machine, Hogget gazed out of the window. He saw the pig chasing chickens. And while he watched, Babe carefully separated the white hens from the brown, just as he'd seen Fly shed certain sheep from the flock.

'Funny, that,' Hogget muttered.

Hogget didn't tell his family, but the next morning he decided to find out if he'd really seen a pig herding chickens! 'Come, Rex. Come, Fly,' he called to his dogs. 'Come, Pig.'

Babe hesitated. Could the Boss really be calling him to work?

'Come, Pig,' Hogget repeated.

Rex tried to hide his shock as Babe followed the dogs through Hogget's automatic sheepgate.

'I expect it's because he's so pleased with what you did yesterday,' Fly whispered.

'Can I learn how to work with sheep today?' Babe asked.

Fly laughed. 'Maybe the Boss will let you watch.'

Babe did watch, very carefully, as Fly and Rex circled the flock of sheep. The dogs barked fiercely and nipped at woolly flanks. The panicked sheep ran through a gate into the sorting yard.

'That'll do,' Hogget said. He sharpened his shears.

Fly dropped, panting, beside Babe as the Boss began clipping wool.

'You're so quick,' Babe said to Fly. 'I'll never be that fast!'

'Speed isn't the thing,' Fly replied. 'It's attitude. The sheep have to know who's boss.'

The sheep looked small and funny without their woolly coats. Hogget looked up from a mountain of greasy wool. 'Get 'em up, Pig.'

Rex stiffened. Fly's mouth gaped. Babe wasn't sure what to do. Then Hogget held open the gate and said, 'Away to me, Pig!'

Fly whispered, 'He wants you to drive them out of the yard. Remember, you have to dominate them.'

Babe trotted to the rear of the flock. He snorted and squealed, trying to bark like a dog. The sheep laughed. The harder Babe tried, the more they laughed.

Babe was discouraged, but Fly said all he needed to do was be mean to the stupid sheep and make them listen to him. Babe tried. But the truth was, he didn't have a mean bone in his body. And the sheep could tell.

Maa bleated, 'What's got into you, young 'un? I just finished tellin' what a nice young chap you be!'

Babe hung his head sheepishly. 'I'm sorry, Maa. I wanted to be a sheepdog.'

''Nuff wolves in the world already without a nice chap like you turnin' nasty,' Maa bleated. 'You haven't got it in you.'

The other sheep agreed, while Rex fumed at Fly. Had she forgotten that they came from a long line of sheepdogs? The very idea of a pig trying to herd sheep was an outrage!

Meanwhile, Babe was busy apologizing to the sheep for his rude behaviour.

'See?' Maa said to the other sheep. 'A heart of gold!' She turned back to Babe. 'No need for all this wolf nonsense. All a nice little chap like you need do is ask.'

Hogget turned away. He was starting to think that maybe his imagination had run away with him. Then Fly barked urgently. Hogget and Rex turned around and saw the entire flock marching like soldiers in a parade, shoulder to shoulder in perfect order. Behind them was the pig, grunting quietly.

Of course, Hogget couldn't hear what Babe was saying. 'Thanks very much. So kind of you. That's right, ladies. Step lively, but no need to rush.'

The sheep bleated happily. 'A pleasure! What a nice chap!'

The farmer was no less amazed than Fly, who peppered Babe with questions. 'How did you do it?'

'I just spoke to them,' Babe said.

Fly couldn't believe it. But Babe stuck to his story.

Rex *really* couldn't believe it. He was furious! When Fly tried to calm him down, Rex attacked her!

Hogget heard the angry yelps and growls of the fighting dogs and rushed to pull them apart. Rex bit the Boss! Fly froze, stunned. Rex had committed the worst possible crime for a dog.

Rex was chained to a spike in the yard. Babe felt awful. Fly was hurt. Rex, the once-proud king of the farm, was in trouble. And the poor little pig couldn't help feeling it was all his fault. He tried to apologize to Rex, but got a bite on the snout for his trouble.

Farmer Hogget called the vet, who stitched Fly's foreleg, put iodine on Babe's snout, and even dressed the wound on Hogget's hand. Then he turned his attention to the worst problem of all – Rex.

'It's not distemper,' the vet said, 'or rabies, so it must be hormones.'

'What about my husband's notion that the dog is jealous of the little pig?' Mrs Hogget asked.

The vet shook his head. 'No, missus. It's the hormones. They'll make a male dog mean. You can keep him locked up or I can do him Tuesday.' He made a snipping sound.

Hogget just said, 'No.'

'Wednesday?' the vet prompted.

Mrs Hogget knew her husband's mind. 'Hogget doesn't want Rex neutered. He's a breeding dog.'

So the vet gave Rex an injection to quieten him down. But that didn't solve Hogget's problems. He tried to give Maa her medicine, but without a dog the farmer couldn't tend the sick sheep. He still needed a sheepdog! Not knowing what else to do, Hogget called for Babe.

'Maa,' said Babe gently, 'the Boss has to give you some medicine.'

'Oh, dear,' Maa bleated, 'I thought so. 'Tis horrible stuff.'

'But it's for the best,' Babe explained.

'Oh, ar, young 'un,' Maa said with a sigh. 'If you say so.'

And with that the old sheep walked right up to Hogget and took her medicine, easy as you please.

Now, a pig doing the work of a sheepdog seemed like a complete miracle to Farmer Hogget. He couldn't deny what he had seen with his own eyes. In the fertile field of his imagination, his daydream quickly grew into

a definite plan. He would take Babe to the trials!

That afternoon Hogget took Fly and Babe to a field bustling with sheepdogs and Bosses and important-looking men with clipboards.

'What are we going to do, Mum?' Babe asked Fly.

'We're not going to do anything,' Fly said. 'I think the Boss wants you to see the trials.' She nodded towards the field.

'What're trials?' Babe asked.

'It's a contest for sheepdogs and their Bosses,' Fly explained. 'You have to fetch five sheep and move them through the gates with the red flags.

You take them down to a circle marked out in the field, and then you have to separate the ones wearing collars from the rest of the flock. Then you gather them all again and herd them into a pen. For a sheepdog there's no prouder moment than that.'

'How do they decide who wins?' Babe asked.

'Time and mistakes,' Fly replied. 'You get points for how quick you are, and you lose points for every twaddle. Every time a sheep goes the wrong way, that's a twaddle.'

At the end of the day, Hogget, Babe, and Fly got back into the lorry.

'Even the champion had a lot of twaddles today,' Babe observed. 'He

would have done better if he'd spoken nicely to the sheep.'

Fly sighed. She loved Babe, but he would go on about those stupid sheep.

'Rex was a champion, wasn't he?' Babe asked.

'He could have been the greatest champion of them all,' Fly said. 'But once, long ago, there was a terrible flood. Rex rounded up some strays. But the sheep were trapped by the rising waters and too stupid and afraid to save their own skins. Rex tried to rescue them. He stayed at the river all night. By morning, they were drowned and Rex was barely alive.'

'Oh, Mum,' Babe gasped.

'Two weeks in front of a cosy fire saw him back on his feet, but he's been almost deaf ever since,' Fly said sadly. 'No one else knows. The worst part is it happened a month before the Grand National Challenge. He couldn't hear the Boss's calls and lost to a dog he'd always beaten.' Fly shook her head. 'If not for the stupidity of sheep, Rex would have been the champion of champions.'

The lorry stopped in the yard. Rex lay in the dust, too groggy even to chase away the duck nibbling his tail.

The very next day, Hogget built a training course for Babe. Mrs Hogget began to worry about her husband. With a farm to run and serious matters to address, he was playing games with a pig. But Farmer Hogget knew that little ideas that tickled and nagged and refused to go away should never be ignored. For in them lie the seeds of destiny.

From the moment Hogget said, 'Away to me, Pig!' to the day's

last 'That'll do', Babe was as eager a sheepdog as ever there was.

In fact, Babe was so eager, he tried to get the cockerel to crow early the next day. The bird shooed him away. So Babe trotted out to the fields in the fuzzy predawn light.

*'Wolf! Wolf!'*

Babe heard terrified bleating. He ran to the aid of the flock. There were sheep tangled in the fence wire. The rest ran to and fro with three wild dogs snapping at their heels. The growling dogs pulled down a ewe.

When the Christmas Eve rustlers came, Babe had felt fear mixed with anger. Now an unfamiliar emotion filled him, a deep and terrible rage.

Babe charged the nearest wild dog and knocked it on its side. The next one he bit as hard as he could. Babe tasted blood.

All three dogs ran howling away with their tails between their shaking legs. Babe chased them to the far fence.

When he was sure they were gone, Babe turned back to the frightened flock, which was gathered around the fallen ewe. 'Maa! Are you all right?' Babe asked when he recognized her.

'Hello, young 'un,' the old sheep said weakly.

Babe licked Maa's wounded neck. Blood smeared his snout. 'You'll be OK. I'll get the Boss up here to look after you.'

'Oh, ar,' Maa said. But her eyes were far away. Her head drooped and life left her. Babe choked back sobs as the Boss's truck rumbled up.

Hogget, Rex, and Fly saw Babe's bloody snout. 'Home, Pig,' Hogget said, his voice quiet and cold.

Fly could not meet Babe's eyes. Rex told her, 'Surely, madam, you can see now that we can't meddle with the natural order. The pig's a killer.'

Fly couldn't believe that was true. So the sheepdog did something she had never done in her long life. Fly talked to the flock. She decided to speak very slowly, for it was a cold fact of nature that sheep were very stupid. 'Did...the...pig...chase...the...sheep?'

The sheep were still shaken from their encounter with the wild dogs. They paid no attention to Fly. She tried bullying them, but that only made them more nervous. At last, she spoke the one word that changed their minds. 'Please. Would you be so kind as to tell me what happened this morning?'

The sheep were stunned to hear a wolf say 'please'. And finally one answered Fly. The sheep spoke very slowly, for it was a cold fact of nature that wolves were ignorant as well as mean. 'Our Baaaa-abe came! He saaaaved us! The wolves killed Maa-aaa, but Babe drove them aw-aaaay!'

Fly sighed with relief. Her boy was not a killer. He was a hero!

'Thank you!' Fly said. But she was already running. Somehow, she had to save Babe!

Babe stared up at the long metal tubes in the Boss's hands. The pig had a vague memory that shiny metal tubes produced food, and he guessed that some treat would come out of the two small round mouths. Well, some kind of surprise, since the Boss levelled the tubes not at Babe's mouth, but at his pink head.

The Boss didn't seem to want to give him the surprise. He stopped to listen to a ringing in the house and to Fly's frantic barking. He slowly turned back to his task when his wife called out 'Hooo-eee! Hogget! Where are you, Arthur?'

Hogget listened to his wife telling him what she'd learned over the phone. Wild dogs were ravaging nearby farms. Hogget unloaded the gun and smiled to himself. The man who never used two words when one would do couldn't help himself. 'Good Pig,' he said. 'Good, good Pig.'

On the rainy day Mrs Hogget left for the Country Women's Association trip, she was a storm of words. She had all kinds of instructions for Mr Hogget, mostly about what to feed himself and what to feed all the animals on the farm.

Hogget carried her suitcase and listened without saying a word. He waved as she rode away on the minibus. Mrs Hogget was a little worried about what her husband would do all alone. But she told herself that even a dreamer like Hogget couldn't get into too much trouble in just three days.

She would have been dismayed indeed to see the farmer let Babe into the house to rest by the fire. But she couldn't have been more upset than Duchess the cat. As soon as Babe settled into a peaceful nap, Duchess slinked up and scratched him on the snout. Babe woke to a hissing, bristling enemy poised to attack again. But Hogget stepped between them.

'Enough,' he said. Then he tossed the cat out into the rain.

Not since Rex had Arthur Hogget had an animal in whose abilities he had so much faith. With the National Grand Challenge Sheepdog Trials only two days away, he wasn't going to let the fact that his animal was a pig stand in his way.

So he took out his rulebook and read it from cover to cover. Then he filled out an entry form. Ever a truthful man, Hogget had worried that the form might say 'Name of Dog'. In which case, whatever he wrote would be a lie. But luck was with him. For the form merely said, 'Name of Entry'. Hogget wrote PIG. Then he used the wondrous Christmas gift from his daughter and faxed the form to the contest.

Meanwhile, in the farmyard, a scrawny, bedraggled bird landed in a puddle. Ferdinand the duck looked even worse than usual. All the animals gathered around him, eager to hear about his adventure. 'Everywhere I went, humans were gunning for me. *Bang! Bang! Bang!* Nowhere to go. Nowhere to hide. Here, at least a feller's got a sporting chance...'

He looked around the yard, realizing that someone was missing. '...Unless, of course, you have the bad luck to be a pig.'

The other animals laughed. Ferdinand didn't know why, until he peered through the living-room window. There was Hogget happily watching TV with Fly and Babe!

Suddenly there was a bright flash of lightning and a huge clap of thunder. The TV went black and all the lights went out. Hogget checked the fuse box, but that wasn't the trouble. So he decided to go to bed.

Fly suggested that Babe get some sleep, too. 'You'll need to be on top form tomorrow.'

Babe snuggled closer to the fire and said, ''Night, Mum.'

The little pig slept, but he had bad dreams. He woke on the morning of the Nationals with a bit of a cold and feeling quite nervous.

Things did not improve at the field of competition. The weather was gloomy. And as the Boss took him to the sheep pen on a lead, Babe couldn't help noticing how many people stared.

Babe took a deep breath and addressed the strange sheep. 'Um...excuse me, sheep...'

The animals did not even look up from their feed.

'Good morning, everyone, my name's Babe!' he called.

The sheep still ignored him. But one turned to see the source of the sound. Babe gasped. The sheep's face was completely black, with a most unfriendly expression. She didn't look like any sheep he had ever seen.

'*Baaaaa,*' the sheep bleated.

Babe tried again. 'I've never met a sheep with such a strong, dark face.'

Now all the other sheep looked at Babe. They were all as unfriendly as the first.

Fly pushed in front of Babe and shouted at the sheep. 'All right, block-heads! Pay attention to what this pig has to say or I'll come in there and rip you to shreds!'

This only made the sheep nervous. 'Wolf! *Baaaa!* Wolf!'

Fly sighed. 'I hadn't expected this.'

Babe's stomach lurched. 'The Boss'll look like a terrible fool if the sheep won't talk to me.'

Fly's furry brow knotted with thought. 'Have to go. I'll try to be back in time.'

Then she went off as fast as she could. Rex stopped her on her way out of the fairground. When Fly told him her plan, he said, 'You can't make it, but I can.'

Fly was surprised. 'But you...you...'

'Don't worry,' the old dog said. 'I won't let the little feller down.' And with that, Rex turned into a blur of speeding fur.

While Rex was gone, Fly, Babe, and Hogget watched the other competitors run their trials. Mrs Hogget also watched the trials on TV with the other Country Women. The ground was slippery with mud, and even the best dogs had many twaddles.

Finally, Rex reached Hogget's farm.

'Wolf! Wolf! Wolf!' cried the sheep in alarm.

Rex had no time for the fears of stupid sheep.

'Shut up, you fools!' he barked breathlessly. 'The little pig's in trouble.'

'Baa-a-abe! Baa-a-aaabe!' the sheep bleated.

'The sheep at the trials won't talk to the little feller. He doesn't know what to do,' Rex explained.

The flock murmured in confusion. Some thought it was wrong to help a wolf, even if the wolf was trying to help Babe. But finally their love for the little pig won out.

'Wait here, wolf,' said an old sheep.

Rex swallowed his pride and said, 'I'm sorry. You'll have to speak up. I'm...a little...hard of hearing.'

The sheep bleated louder, 'I asked you to wait here, wolf. Do what you're told by an old sheep for a change, and we'll see what we can do for you.'

Rex waited while the sheep came up with a plan. Finally, the old sheep turned to Rex and said, 'We've got something that might help Babe. But us sheep don't like giving it to no wolf.'

'Paaa-a-assword!' several bleated.

Before they would give Rex the password, the sheep made him promise to treat them nicely and politely and not to bite them, and most of all never to use the password to harm another sheep in any way.

'I promise you that,' Rex said solemnly. 'I'll make sure the pig knows it, too. Don't you worry. The password is safe with me.'

The password was something every sheep learned when it was just a little lamb. Even now, the sheep hesitated to tell it to Rex. But one said, ''Tis for Babe's sa-aaa-ke. Maa would have waaanted it.' That silenced all the objections.

Rex repeated the password to himself over and over as he raced back to the fair. He dodged madly through the crowd to get to the trial area. Rex heard the announcer say, 'The last entry is "Pig", owner A. Hogget.'

Mrs Hogget heard the name but could not believe it. 'That must be a different Hogget,' she told her friends. 'We've only got the two dogs and they certainly aren't...' Something terrible occurred to her then. He couldn't! No, he wouldn't!

At that same moment, the contest officials were saying, 'But you can't! We'd be the laughing stock of every sheepdog organization in the world!'

But the rulebook had nothing against pigs running in the trials. So the committee finally agreed to let Hogget run Babe.

The crowd gasped and giggled when the little pig came out on the field. Mrs Hogget fainted. Having received the password from Rex, Fly ran past the officials to tell Babe.

The TV announcer joked, 'Perhaps the dog's giving the pig a few pointers on how to be a "sheep-pig"!'

Then the clock started and Hogget said, 'Away to me, Pig.'

Babe waddled to meet the six black-faced sheep in the field. The crowd laughed while Babe squealed the password: 'Baa-a Ram Ewe, baa-a-a Ram Ewe, each lamb can hold the wisdom of the Gra-a-and Ram Ewe.'

The sheep were stunned to hear a pig speak the password. 'Fancy him knowing the pa-a-a-assword!'

Now that he had their attention, Babe said, 'And a very good afternoon to you all. I do apologize for having to ask you to do work in this truly miserable weather. I hope you'll forgive me.'

The sheep were so pleased by Babe's lovely manners that, of course, they did exactly what he asked. Without so much as one twaddle they marched

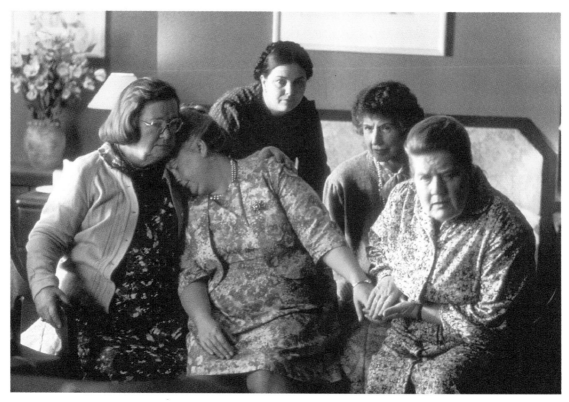

neatly through the course. The jokes and laughter died into a stunned silence. Even the TV announcers were struck dumb.

But Babe wasn't. He carefully instructed the sheep on how to finish the course. And they gladly obliged. At the last gate, the shed sheep rejoined the rest of the flock. And they all marched into the final pen. Then Hogget closed the gate.

The crowd erupted in thunderous applause and cheers. Babe had a perfect score. No sheepdog had ever got a perfect score at the National Grand Challenge Sheepdog Trials. But this amazing sheep-pig did!

At that moment, on the Hoggets' farm, the power was restored. The TV set clicked on, and the animals in the yard heard wild cheering. They all looked through the window and saw Babe on TV.

Ferdinand could hardly believe his eyes. 'A perfect score! The pig's done it!' he shouted to the flock. 'Hooray for Babe the Gallant Pig!'

'Aaaaar! Our Ba-aaa-abe! Hoora-a-a-ay!' the sheep bleated.

But in all the celebration and hubbub of noise and excitement, two figures were silent and still, side by side. Though every single human in

the stands and commentary boxes was at a complete loss for words, the man who, in his life, had uttered fewer words than any of them knew exactly what to say.

Hogget looked down at Babe and said, 'That'll do, Pig.'

Babe turned his bright eyes up to his Boss.

Hogget repeated softly, 'That'll do.'